## AUTHOR'S NOTE

*Girl Wonder* was inspired by the life of baseball pioneer Alta Weiss, born February 9, 1890, in Ragersville, Ohio. In 1907, at age seventeen, Alta pitched for a semipro all-male team, the Vermilion Independents. The next season her father became a co-owner, and it was renamed the Weiss All-Stars. Alta went on to become a doctor, graduating in 1914 from Starling-Ohio Medical College (a predecessor to the Ohio State University College of Medicine) in Columbus, the only woman in her class. She died in 1964.

For more information on Alta Weiss, see *Women at Play* by Barbara Gregorich (Harcourt Brace, 1993). The National Baseball Hall of Fame and Museum Web site at www.baseballhalloffame.org has a bibliography on women and baseball. For information about women's baseball today, see www.womenplayingbaseball.com.

## ACKNOWLEDGMENTS

Special thanks to Tim Wiles, director of research at the National Baseball Hall of Fame and Museum, and to Ray Hisrich for permission to use the photos of his great aunt, Alta Weiss. Thank you to the Baseball Hall of Fame for use of the photograph that appears on the jacket of this book.

ALADDIN PAPERBACKS
An imprint of Simon & Schuster Children's Publishing Division
1230 Avenue of the Americas, New York, NY 10020
Text copyright © 2003 by Deborah Hopkinson
Illustrations copyright © 2003 by Terry Widener
All rights reserved, including the right of reproduction
in whole or in part in any form.
ALADDIN PAPERBACKS and colophon are
trademarks of Simon & Schuster, Inc.
Also available in an Atheneum Books for Young Readers hardcover edition.
Designed by Ann Bobco and Terry Widener
Hand lettering and border design by Chris Costello
The text of this book was set in Triplex Serif.
The illustrations for this book were rendered in acrylic paint.
Manufactured in China
First Aladdin Paperbacks edition March 2006
14 16 18 20 19 17 15
The Library of Congress has cataloged the hardcover edition as follows:
Hopkinsons, Deborah.
Girl Wonder: a baseball story in nine innings /
by Deborah Hopkinson ; illustrated by Terry Widener.—1st ed.
p. cm.
Summary: In the early 1900s, Alta Weiss, a young woman who knows
from an early age that she loves baseball, finds a way that she
can play, even though she is a girl.
ISBN 978-0-689-83300-7 (hc.)
1. Weiss, Alta, 1890-1964—Juvenile fiction. [1. Weiss, Alta, 1890-1964—Fiction.
2. Baseball—Fiction.] I. Widener, Terry, ill. II. Title.
PZ7.H778125 Gi 2003
[E]—dc21
99-047052
ISBN-13: 978-1-4169-1393-1 (pbk.)
ISBN-10: 1-4169-1393-9 (pbk.)
0819 SCP

# GIRL WONDER

## A Baseball Story in Nine Innings

### by DEBORAH HOPKINSON
with pictures by TERRY WIDENER

Aladdin Paperbacks
NEW YORK   LONDON   TORONTO   SYDNEY

I must have been born to play baseball,

because Pop says I was only two

when I hurled a corncob at an old tomcat

chasing my favorite hen.

They say I threw so hard,

that cob shot across the barnyard

and bopped him on the head.

John, the handyman, whistled in surprise.

"Wouldja look at that, Doc?" he said to Pop.

"Your little girl's got some arm on her."

And that old cat?

He leaped like lightning,

and never pestered my chickens again.

My own first memory

is of John tossing a baseball to me,

the glove on my hand as big

as one of Mama's prize sunflowers.


Somehow, even then, I could make

that hard, round ball zing through the air.

By the time I was six I'd throw for hours.

Pop pinned a target on a bale of hay and told me,

"Get ready, wind up, let 'er fly!"

Most times I'd hit the bull's-eye,

while John and Pop just shook their heads and exclaimed,

"Alta, you're a real Girl Wonder."

Nothing could keep me from baseball.

Summers I played with the boys in town.

And even in winter I got up early to practice.

Oh, that barn was icy.

The cows breathed frosty puffs into the air

as they turned their saucer eyes to watch me—

my first fans!

But the bitter Ohio cold

couldn't put out the fire inside me.

I threw that ball again and again

till all my muscles knew what to do,

as easy as singing my ABCs.

By the time I was seventeen

I'd struck out every boy in town.

"You're almost a lady," said my friends.

"Isn't it time you quit playing games?"

"Quit?" I cried. "I haven't even started!"

Still, every once in a while, I wondered if they might be right.

Then Pop and I took a trip to Vermilion

to see the sights.

I spotted some fellows playing ball on the green.

They looked so sharp, I itched to join 'em.

"Afternoon, gentlemen. Mind if I play?" I asked,

sweet as honey.

"Sure thing, miss," they smirked.

"Don't worry, we'll toss it to you nice and gentle."


Well, I threw that ball back so hard,

their faces glowed beet red with shame

and their hands must've stung right through their gloves.

"Wow!" they cried, shaking their heads.

"You should play for the Independents,

our town's semipro team."

"Where do I sign up?" I replied.

When the Independents' crusty old coach

took one look at my long, blue skirt,

he spit hard on the ground.

"Go home, missy. You're a girl—

and this is baseball."

Go home? Not a chance.

Suddenly I grabbed on to an idea.

"Just sign me up, Coach," I said, smiling sweetly.

"And as sure as 'Strike Out' is my middle name,

I guarantee you'll sell lots of tickets.

Folks are curious to see a girl play."

The coach pulled down his cap,

but not before I saw his eyes light up

like he'd just hit a home run out of the park.

I could read his line of thinking,

clear as a catcher's signs:

*Girls can't throw.*

*Girls can't play baseball.*

*But this gal just might bring in some dough.*

At last he stuck out his hand.

"It's a deal, Miss Weiss.

You got one chance to show your stuff.

But you better not make a fool of me."

Finally, the big game.

The stands are full. The whole town's here.

Coach wipes the sweat from his face.

"Sure you don't want to play right field?"

But I'm already on my way to the mound.

The crowd leans forward.

Are folks on my side

or just itching to hiss and jeer?

## Play ball!

The first batter's big—a mean, glaring bull.

For a flash I panic; maybe Coach is right.

My pitch is wide. Ball one.

The fans twitter. I shake off my nerves,

crack my chewing gum, and stare him down.

Now I'm even when he fans—

one ball, one strike.

Inside on the next, just barely—

two balls, one strike.

I chance the outside corner.

*Whoosh!* The big bull cuts the air—we're even again.

The crowd buzzes.

I try my knuckler next, but it drops too low—

three balls, two strikes. Full count.

The batter's surprised I've gotten this far.

He digs in, mad.

The crowd falls silent, all eyes on me.

"No different from my fans in the barn,"

I tell myself.

I reach inside and pull out my best stuff;

I always did have a pretty fair fastball.

*Crack!* He hits it!

Looks like a sizzling line drive, a sure base hit.

But wait—it rockets right to me,

and my glove's in the air, quick as light.

Got it! He's out!

The place explodes with cheers.

"Nice catch, Girl Wonder!"

And from the dugout I hear Coach yell,

"Didn't I always say she could do it?"

I smile. I've never had so much fun.

I nod to my teammates.

"One down, two to go. Let's get 'em, boys."

And I strike the next batter out.

I pitch five innings, then play first base.

The final score is four to three, us.

The Independents win.

We keep winning, too, all summer long.

They even run special trains from Cleveland,

so fans can see the new star pitcher:

*me, the Girl Wonder!*

*The girl who can throw.*

*The girl who can play baseball.*

I played another season,

even pitched in a major league stadium,

and always held my own against the best.

But now my playing days are done.

I'm too busy being a doctor, like Pop.

Only girl in the class of 1914.

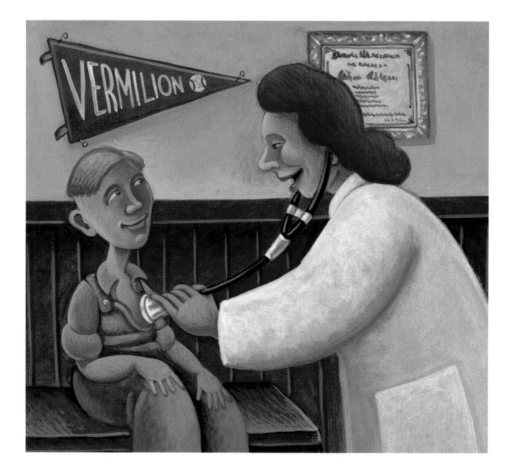

But just the other day I spotted a little gal.

Cap pulled down, overalls full of mud.

"Hey, you with the glove," I yelled. "Come on over.

Did you ever hear the story of the Girl Wonder?"

HIGHLIGHTS OF WOMEN IN BASEBALL

**1866** Newly formed Vassar College has baseball teams with eight players. Other women's colleges soon follow.

**1867** The Dolly Vardens, a black women's team in Philadelphia, becomes the earliest professional women's baseball team.

**1875** Two women's barnstorming teams, the Blondes and the Brunettes, are formed as moneymaking entertainment.

**1897** Early pitching pioneer Maud Nelson plays for the Boston Bloomer Girls. Bloomer Girl teams often included a few men.

**1898** Lizzie Arlington pitches in a regulation minor league game.

**1905** Amanda Clement at age seventeen becomes the first woman paid to umpire a baseball game.

**1907** Alta Weiss pitches for the Vermilion Independents, an Ohio semipro team.

**1911** Maud Nelson forms the Western Bloomer Girls and continues to establish women's touring teams through the 1930s.

**1928** Longtime semipro player Lizzie "Spike" Murphy becomes the first woman to play for a major league team in an exhibition game.

**1934** Olympian Babe Didrikson pitches several major league exhibition games as a promotional gimmick.

**1943** The All-American Girls Professional Baseball League is established and is active until 1954.

**1949** Toni Stone begins playing in the Negro Leagues. In 1953 she gets a hit off the great Satchel Paige.

**1952** Minor leagues prohibit the signing of women.

**1974** Little League baseball is opened to girls, following lawsuits.

**1994** Colorado Silver Bullets, a professional women's team, is formed. Active until 1997.

**2001** Inaugural Women's World Series held in Toronto, Canada.